Donny J Trump is a Great Big Liar!

The Story of a Nice Boy
Struggling with a Moral Deficiency

A work of fiction

incuding *References* to reality

by Sigmund Noetzel

FAULCOURT PRESS

For

Lyla and Aiden

You're never too young
to learn about mendacity.

Once upon a time, a boy named Donny J
had the idea that he was more than okay,
but just the most wonderful boy on earth.
His fantasy was his fantastic worth.

But folks didn't know that he was such a gem,
so what do you think? —he had to tell them.
He shot off his mouth like popping corn,
like a blowhard tooting his very own horn.

His blather was all with himself obsessed,
—the biggest, the greatest, top notch, the best,
and he was the winner in all that he tried.
But it wasn't true, so when he said it, he lied.

He wanted people to know his name
and know who he is –and this is called *fame*.

He wanted them all to be telling his story
because he's so great –and this is called *glory*.

He really wanted —it was his true goal—
them praising *him* for his wonderful soul.

When he told the plain truth, it was not good enough
to make folks adore him, so he made up stuff

that wasn't real, but they didn't know;
he made them believe, by saying it was so.

Playing make-believe is fun
when the game is played by everyone.

But Donny makes people believe
what's really not so; it's called *deceive*.

It's not the same as playing a game.
It's not fun for everyone; it shouldn't be done.

I'm building a really great castle!

Believe me.

Nobody builds a castle better than me!

You're just digging holes

and filling them in!

Lying is a sin!

Even though Donny had a lot of stuff,
he never seemed to have enough
to make people see he was the cat's meow,
for that is what he thought, everyhow.

So he thought if *they* thought he had a lot of money,
they would love him for it, and life would be sunny.
So he lied, and said he had a whole lot.
He kept hidden the truth, that he really did not.

But he lies, and people did know it.
If he had so much money, they told him to show it.
But he couldn't —and for a reason why,
he made up another stupid lie.

Whatever I wanted,
I could've bought it.

But I can't
show my money—
it's under Audit!

Donny loves himself so very much,
different people he won't even touch.
People who don't look like him,
different size or shape or color of skin,

people not rich, or less than first-rate;
these are people he likes to hate.
That he hates he will always deny,
but watch what he does, you'll see it's a lie.

Those kids are not from here,

and they're very, very,

horribly bad!

Donny J aways has to boast
about being the best and having the most,
and everything about him is super size.
It's just a lot of stupid lies.

Some people know it, and might even choose
to tell us all, to spread the news.
But to make sure that they will not try it,
Donny pays them money to keep quiet.

That's my school.
Believe me, it's the best!

That's what you say.

But let's ask the kids
coming this way.

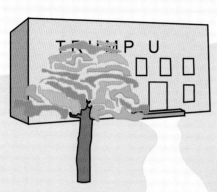

I think you made a big mistake.
Your school is nothing but a fake!

Don't be fooled
by their crying.
Those kids are lying!

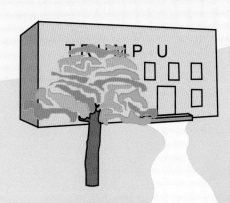

Is eveyone lying except for you?
They're going to Sue,
Donny, what will you do?

I'll have to give
them some money,
then you will see,
they will stop telling
bad lies about me!

You would think that a boy with a talent for lies
would be able to see in another's eyes
that he's a liar too.
You would think that, wouldn't you?

You would think, hard and long,
And you would be wrong.

I asked him once, I asked him twice,
He answered me so very nice,
the same answer every time.
So it's the truth, like lines that rhyme.

He's like your
little big brother.
Do you lie
to each other?

When his lies are exposed by what he does,
he'll change his behavior; deny what he was.

He'll simply create alternative facts,
with phony behavior and unnatural acts.

When people tell what they know is true
about the things he really does do,

but Donny has said otherwise
when he told his made-up lies,

then he must lie some more,
and like a lying lion roar

that *they're* the ones that are lying.

Yes, they're lying! Those girls are fat and ugly witches, who only want some of my riches.

You're not much of a classy guy—

a nasty mouth, with the nasty lie!

He thinks he himself is the center of all;
what he says will tell us what's up on the wall.

You can believe what you see with your own eyes,
Or else believe Donny Trump's lies.

Here are the tacks.
Ours are red, white and blue.

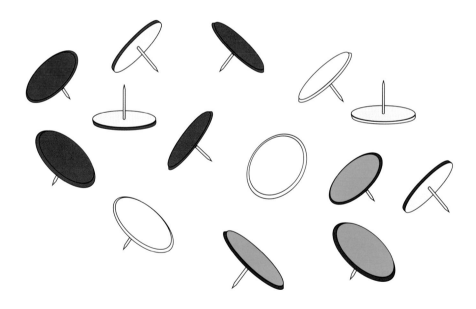

All of the tacks are put up on the wall.

Lies make enemies; the lie-believers
set against the truth-perceivers,

who call out the lies in no uncertain terms
—which only opens a can of worms.

Would the lie-believers like to admit
to being fooled? Not one little bit!

A hint of the truth brings a troubled frown
and a search for a way to double down,

to find some angle from which to twist
the facts, then on just that, insist.

Or they'll look beyond the lie
to find not the truth, but a reason why

the facts are trumped by some matter higher,
on which they line up on the side of the liar.

The lie is not then judged by facts,
but appeals to emotion, determining acts.

When a lie stirs up the spirit of fear,
your truth is whatever you need to hear.

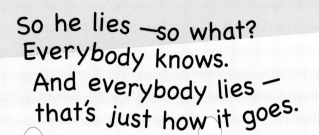

So he lies —so what?
Everybody knows.
And everybody lies —
that's just how it goes.

They're only lies
because
they confuse
the bad guys
with the
fake news!

No one in
this neighborhood
really believes
that lying is good!

And Donny lived happily ever after.
Just kidding! Ha, ha! (the sound of laughter).

Kidding is when it's not true what you say,
but then you tell the truth right away

and turn it all around,
and make that ha-ha sound.

But no kidding now, this is for real,
"happily ever after" isn't in Donny's deal,

'cause Donny won't be happy till his lies become truth,
till people will say, "My, what a fine youth,

so clear-eyed and honest, decisive and bold,
so noble, so clever —the truth be told—

so smart, so strong, so never-ever wrong,
so handsome, iconic, a brow so Teutonic,

so Aryan white, gut instincts so right,
so genetically endowed, so properly proud,

so leonine of mane, so winning of name,
with mind so brilliant, tenacious, resilient,

so agile, elastic —his genius fantastic!

deserving just deserts, deliciously edible,
his insights are just mostly incredible!

Conceptions inconceivable —perceptions unbelievable!

And stable —so stable! Don't take that off the table!

He's got this, if anything's true —stability out the gazoo!

Stability beyond belief,
in spite of the negative press covfefe

The fat cats on the Street will gather at his feet,
feign taking abuse, then put him to use.

Even Jellicle cats will lift their hats

to his fabled piles of lucre, which surely attest
that he has by their deity been richly blessed

(and for these good folk, an inside joke;
two Corinthians walk into a bar...)

This boy will be a stand-up star,

a lady's enchanter with his locker-room banter,
a master debater, an immigrant hater,

so tweetful a feller, an exceptional speller,
so full of mirth, so certified of birth,

it must be told, such a heart for gold,
so *sui generis*, so very one-of-a kind,

so oh so healthy in his body and his mind,
with all of his urges and passions aligned,

a synecdoche of a maga nation,
a hive-mind united in adulation

where you'll see the people rise,
sing his praises to the skies,

one nation, visible sans schism
in the prism of his narcissism,

and the sycophantization of the whole population
congeals in an orgy of solipsization…"

Whoa! I think we got carried away!
We only needed to say—

the lesson that Donny's story will teach
is that happiness will be out of reach,

no matter how hard somebody tries,
if that person's life is based on lies.

The end of this story will likely be bad,
with a final tweet that ends in
Sad.

REFERENCES

TOWER
The Trump Tower on Fifth Ave., which Trump has advertised to the world and prospective tenants as a 68-story building, is actually 58 stories, as listed in the NYC Department of Buildings. ["By Fudging Math, Trump Takes His Towers to Greater Heights," Vivian Lee, New York Times, Nov. 2, 2016.] Although it is now common for condominium towers to exaggerate their height, Trump is proud to take credit for initiating the practice: "They all follow my lead."

BEACH
In Chapter 8 of "Art of the Deal" (by Donald J. Trump and Tony Schwartz), Trump reveals how he deceived the Board of Directors of a company that was considering investing with him in a building project. He had acquired the building site, and the Board was coming to Atlantic City to evaluate the progress of the project. But construction had not yet begun, so Trump ordered bulldozers and dump trucks to the site to dig holes and move dirt around to give the appearance of building activity while the Board was in town.

Trump writes that he had discussed the project with the company's CEO, but he does not explain why the Board would then have believed that construction had begun.

One board member asked Trump why a bulldozer was filling in a hole it had just dug. "That was difficult for me to answer," Trump writes, but does not reveal how he answered. Telling the truth would have negated the entire deception.

Of course, Trump does not use the word deception. He prefers 'gaming.'

AUDIT
During the first debate with Hillary Clinton, Trump asserted that he couldn't release his tax return because it's under audit. The reasoning is a lie: an audit does not in any way prevent a tax return from becoming public. The moderators pointed this out; Trump ignored it, and asserted, "as soon as the audit's finished, it will be released." This was another lie: it's not being released. [https://www.washingtonpost.com/news/the-fix/wp/2016/09/26/the-first-trump-clinton-presidential-debate-transcript-annotated/?utm_term=.2b5e16e07ad5]

KIDS
In 1989, a young woman jogging in New York City's Central Park was brutally assaulted and raped. While the victim was in a coma, five teenagers were charged in the attack, and Donald Trump, a private citizen with no record of advocacy for social justice, took out full-page ads in the New York Times and the Daily News, advocating the death penalty. His ad did not specifically mention the accused teenagers, but railed against a "dangerously permissive atmosphere which allows criminals of every age to beat and rape a helpless woman..." Trump also wrote, "Mayor Koch has stated that hate and rancor should be removed from our hearts. I do not think so. I want to hate these muggers and murderers." [Daily News, May 1,1989. See http://assets.nydailynews.com/polopoly_fs/1.1838466.1403324800!/img/httpImage/image.jpg_gen/derivatives/article_970/trump21n-1-web.jpg?enlarged]

Then in a televised interview with Larry King, Trump stated, ""maybe hate is what we need if we're going to get anything done." [https://www.cnn.com/2016/10/07/politics/trump-larry-king-central-park-five/]

Trump had no more than publicly available information about the crime. Why was he so certain of the guilt of the accused? One can only speculate. Four of the teenagers were African-American and one Hispanic.

The youths confessed to the crime, but later attempted to rescind their confessions, claiming they were forced. And even though the DNA sample collected at the crime scene did not match any of theirs, they were convicted and sentenced to long prison terms. Years later, in 2002, they were exonerated as a convicted murderer and rapist confessed to the crime; his confession was corroborated by the DNA evidence. The convicted youths sued the city, and, in 2014, were awarded a $41 million settlement.

Trump wrote an outraged op-ed in the NY Daily News opposing this payment. Of the teenagers who spent years in jail for a crime they did not commit, he wrote, "The recipients must be laughing out loud at the stupidity of the city." And, ignoring their demonstrated innocence and the lack of any previous arrest record, he argues, "Speak to the detectives on the case and try listening to the facts. These young men do not exactly have the pasts of angels." He presents no facts, only accusations. [http://www.nydailynews.com/new-york/nyc-crime/donald-trump-central-park-settlement-disgrace-article-1.1838467]

He also asked, rhetorically, "If they were innocent, why did they confess?" Possibly, these fourteen to sixteen-year olds might have come to believe, under police interrogation, that the victim was going to die, and they would face the death penalty, unless they confessed to the crime. Demand for the death penalty was the main message of Trump's ad.

In his June 2015 speech announcing his candidacy, Trump again made unsubstantiated accusations of rape by minorities, "When Mexico sends its people, they're not sending the best.... They're bringing drugs, they're bringing crime. They're rapists and some, I assume, are good people." [http://time.com/3923128/donald-trump-announcement-speech/] To assert that Mexico is "sending" people is the first lie. The immigrants are poor people seeking better economic advantages in the US; Mexico is not *sending* them.

The second lie is that they are rapists. Government statistics show that the crime rate among illegal immigrants is lower than that of citizens. [Contrary to Trump's Claims, Immigrants Are Less Likely to Commit Crimes, By Richard Perez-Pena, Jan. 26, 2017] [Reports find that immigrants commit less crime than US-born citizens. by Rafael Bernal - 03/19/17, http://thehill.com/]

Trump's claim is no ordinary lie, but a ploy used by demagogues throughout history: stir up fear and hatred of foreigners and minorities, and announce yourself as the only one that can protect the people from them. As one example —not at all the only one— a demagogic twenthiest century politician used this technique to agitate the German people against the Jews, which brought him enough political support to finally overthrow Germany's democracy without ever achieving a majority vote. Trump cannot be accused of anti-Semitism; his beloved daughter has converted to Judaism, and some major Republican donors are Jews. But throughout his campaign, he has relentlessly stirred fear and anger at the Hispanic, black and Muslim minorities, through lies ("they're rapists") with a veneer of reasonableness ("some, I suppose, are good people").

SCHOOL
Students who paid tens of thousands of dollars to take Real Estate courses at Trump's educational venture, "Trump University," sued the school, claiming it was falsely advertised, and taught them nothing of value. Among the charges of false advertising and high-pressure sales tactics based on deception, there was the falsity of the school's claim that its instructors were "handpicked" by Donald Trump. But when Donald Trump attempted to get himself personally removed from the case, he claimed minimal involvement with the "university" and stated in a deposition that he did not know the instructors. (His motion to be personally excluded was denied because of his almost total ownership and much evidence of deep involvement with the organization.) [http://

A separate legal action initiated by the Attorney General of New York State in 2013 described the multiple reasons why Trump University was operating illegally, and was in fact a sham of an educational institution. [http://online.wsj.com/public/resources/documents/trump.pdf]

Trump settled two class-action lawsuits, in which 3,730 students made claims (about 7600 were eligible), as well as the fraud action by New York State, with a $25 million payment to the victims. By accepting the settlement, the students forfeited their right to any further claims against Trump University. The "university" admitted no wrongdoing. [https://www.npr.org/sections/thetwo-way/2017/03/31/522199535/judge-approves-25-million-settlement-of-trump-university-lawsuit]

VLAD

Throughout the campaign, Trump praised Vladimir Putin, calling him a more effective leader than the US President, and expressing a desire to be like him. The CIA determined that the Russian government meddled in the US election — hacking the Democratic National Committee computer and posting its emails on Wikileaks, and conducting social media campaigns to spread disinformation.

At the G-20 meeting on July 8, 2017, Trump had a two-hour private meeting with Putin. He later described his interaction with Putin as follows: "First question - first 20, 25 minutes - I said, 'Did you do it?' He said, 'No, I did not, absolutely not.' I then asked him a second time, in a totally different way. He said, 'Absolutely not.' ... Somebody did say if he did do it, you wouldn't have found out about it. Which is a very interesting point." [Transcript of Trump interview with Reuters, 7/12/17, at http://reut.rs/2sRVuHc]

In a later interview about that meeting, Trump is quoted as follows: "He said he didn't meddle. I asked him again. You can only ask so many times ... He said he absolutely did not meddle in our election. He did not do what they are saying he did.' " [Washington Post November 11, 2017, 'He said he didn't meddle': Trump talks with Putin about U.S. elections and Syria in brief interactions. By Ashley Parker, David Nakamura and Karen DeYoung]

Trump knows that Putin didn't meddle, because he takes Putin at his word. If Trump is not lying, and actually believes Putin — a man who rose to power in the Soviet KGB, the secret police and spy agency — he is a fool.

FLAG

On several occasions during the campaign, Trump demonstrated a casual attitude towards the flag, neglecting to salute as the National Anthem began to play (or even, as president, saluting only after being prodded by a nudge from his wife.) Of course, saluting the flag is purely a symbolic gesture, and there is no law requiring it. (A point his supporters have made in his defense.)

However, when African-American football players knelt during the National Anthem in protest against institutional racism, Trump opposed them by elevated flag-worship to the highest expression of patriotism, and overcompensated for his former flag-indifference by a crowd-pleasing ritual of flag hugging. [https://www.youtube.com/watch?v=15Qc8h38Rb4] [https://www.youtube.com/watch?v=0q2QUUD-nDEI]

PUSSY

In the Access Hollywood video released by The Washington Post, Donald Trump boasts of groping women, "Yeah, that's her, with the gold. I better use some Tic Tacs just in case I start kissing her. You know, I'm automaticaliy attracted to beautiful — I just start kissing

them. It's like a magnet. Just kiss. I don't even wait. And when you're a star, they let you do it. You can do anything." ... "Grab 'em by the pussy. You can do anything." [https://www.nytimes.com/2016/10/08/us/donald-trump-tape-transcript.html]

After the tape was released, Trump's website posted a video with his response. He admits to the conversation, but calls it "just locker room banter"; apologizes for it "if anyone was offended"; pledges to "be a better man," then demonstrates the character of this better man by attacking Bill Clinton for not only saying "far worse... not even close", but actually abusing women (whereas he only falsely boasted of it); and attacked Hillary for bullying those women. [https://www.youtube.com/watch?v=ycfARBsz6_Y#]

But at least sixteen women have since come forward to assert that in various instances Trump did grope, grab, fondle, caress and kiss them without permission. Two brought lawsuits against him. In every case to which Trump has responded, he dismissed these women as liars, and their accusations as politically motivated. [https://abcnews.go.com/Politics/list-trumps-accusers-allegations-sexual-misconduct/story?id=51956410]

In his campaign rallies, Trump employed a more persuasive argument to refute the accusation of one woman. After a mocking impression of her complaint against him, he uses a sarcastic tone of incredulity, "Yeah, I'm going to go after her." He makes a screwed-up face, then, "Believe me, she would not be my first choice, that I can tell you." He's clearly implying that she's unattractive, which he's offering as proof that she's lying; after all, he could not have been aroused to assault a less than beautiful woman. [https://www.youtube.com/watch?v=bq2zibeZ-xw at 2:14]

TACKS

During the eighth Republican candidates debate, Trump declared, "The United States is the highest taxed country in the world!" And later, again, "... right now, we're the highest taxed country in the world. Under my plan, we cut not only taxes for the middle class, but we cut taxes for corporations." [http://time.com/4210921/republican-debate-transcript-new-hampshire-eighth/] In the tenth debate, he said, "If you look at what's going on, we have the highest taxes anywhere in the world. We pay more business tax, we pay more personal tax. We have the highest taxes in the world." [http://time.com/4238363/republican-debate-tenth-houston-cnn-telemundo-transcript-full-text/] These are absurd lies. The reality is that almost all the developed industrial nations have higher personal tax rates than the United States, a few as much as 50% higher.

It is true that the United States at that time had one of the highest corporate tax rates in the world. But corporations are not *in* any country. The fact that a corporation is registered in the United Simply puts no restriction on where its facilities are, where its employees are, where its markets are, nor where its revenues come from. The largest US-registered corporations are multinational; all facets of their economic activity are worldwide. Nor is their any restriction on where its owners are. About a quarter to a third of the stock value of US corporations is owned by foreigners (so a cut in corporate taxes is largely a tax cut for foreigners).

After Trump became president, his press secretary defended the lies by claiming he was talking about corporate taxes. This is another lie. If one intends to talk about corporate taxes, one simply uses the words "corporate taxes" –as did several of the other candidates in the debate. Trump didn't. He said the "highest taxed country," and then specifically said "personal tax."